ALICE'S
ADVENTURES IN
WONDERLAND

Published by Sourcebooks Wonderland, an Imprint of Sourcebooks Kids.
Sourcebooks and the colophon are registered trademarks of Sourcebooks.
All Rights Reserved.
P.O. Box 4410, Naperville, Illinois 60567-4410
(630) 961-3900
Fax: (630) 961-2168
sourcebooks.com

sesameworkshop.org

Design by Whitney Manger
Craft illustrations by Jenny Bee

Library of Congress data is on file with the publisher.

Printed and bound in the United States of America.
MA 10 9 8 7 6 5 4 3 2 1

ghost writer™

ALICE'S ADVENTURES IN WONDERLAND

by Lewis Carroll

adapted by Olugbemisola Rhuday-Perkovich

illustrated by Erin McGuire

with an introduction by Kwame Alexander

sourcebooks
wonderland

SESAME WORKSHOP.

Dear Rock Star Reader,

Books are like amusement parks, and this one here is a roller coaster. As you begin your reading adventure, I just want to chime in and say get ready for an incredibly amazing experience reimagining some of your favorite books. That's right: between the pages of this book, Ghostwriter is bringing your favorite characters to life to help solve a mystery. How cool is that?

I bet you think that because I'm an author, I love to read. Well, you're right! In order to become a good writer, you gotta be a great reader. Every time you read a meaningful or magical poem or story or really clever post, you're instantly transformed and sometimes transported to new ideas and worlds: sports arenas, foreign lands, outer space, other times in history, and even other kids' lives. But I wasn't always that way.

When I was twelve, I thought reading was uncool. Why? Because my dad chose huge, boring books he thought

I should read. After a few years of that torture, my mom encouraged me to pick out my own books at our local library, and I found my way back to finding reading cool. (I guess you could say I started choosing my own rides at the amusement park.) Then I started reading everything—chapter books, short stories, comic books, biographies, and, of course, poetry. Ghostwriter, like my mom, believes that there's a perfect book for every kid out there. And the one you're reading could be yours.

I love getting lost in a good story, and there are so, so many great stories out there just waiting for you. Our friend Ghostwriter is gonna help you find them—and then rock your world one page at a time.

I thank you for your attention, and I'm outta here!

Kwame Alexander

Poet, Educator, and Newbery Medal-winning author of *The Crossover*

chapter 1

If Alice's sister was anything to go by, being a teenager was boring. It was a Saturday, when they could be figuring out how to turn broccoli into chocolate. They could be playing astronaut with their cat, Dinah. They might practice being invisible! But her sister Serena was…reading a book. A book with no pictures! What was that about?

"You're supposed to play with me," Alice reminded her sister. The park in front of them was filled with grass and flowers and possibility. It was meant for running and laughing, not quietly sitting and reading pictureless books.

Serena looked up. "I told you to bring a book too."

"Mom said, 'Go play,'" Alice replied, rolling her eyes. Everyone knew that anything was better than a boring old storybook.

"What she said exactly was 'Girls, go play.' That pretty much definitely means that *you* are supposed to play with *me*." Alice thought her argument sounded good, even though she was making it up as she went. Then, because she was also smart, she added, "Please?"

Serena sighed and put down her book. "Come here," she said. "I was just reading about a girl who lives on another planet—"

"Space game!" said Alice. "Yay!"

"And she was getting ready to go…on an adventure," said Serena. "So she put on her space outfit."

"Yes?"

"And put her hair in *cosmic queen* braids."

"How are those different from regular braids?" asked Alice. Serena had thick coils that made for easy braiding, but Alice's slippery hair was often

a challenge. She wasn't usually eager to let Serena experiment, but *cosmic queen* braids might be worth it.

"Let's figure it out!" said Serena. She pulled a comb and hair accessories out of her bag and started braiding Alice's hair before Alice could even wonder if she'd been tricked. (She had.)

Oh well, thought Alice a few minutes later as she looked out at a row of dandelions. The sun was bright, and the breeze was light. She settled back as her sister braided. Dandelions were quite beautiful, she realized. Maybe she'd make herself a flower crown and be queen of the space when they were done with this part of the game.

Suddenly, a fluffy white rabbit in a bright blue coat and a blue-and-orange vest darted out from a cluster of bushes.

"Oh no!" he said. "I'm late again! Oh, my ears

and whiskers, she's going to be *furious*!"

Alice sat up straight. Now, this was interesting. Then the White Rabbit took an old-fashioned watch out of its vest pocket and squeaked again. "Oh no! Oh dear, I'm really late! Oh dear, oh no, I've got to go!"

Alice sat up even straighter because, even though everyone knew that animals could talk (most people just didn't listen), she didn't think that many smartly dressed rabbits used their vest pockets for actual pocket watches. Carrots, maybe.

This was too interesting to ignore. As the White Rabbit darted away, Alice jumped up and ran after it, ignoring the comb that fell from her hair. The White Rabbit jumped into a hole, and since just maybe this could end up being even better than playing Space People, Alice jumped in after it.

chapter 2

The tunnel went straight for a long time, and Alice could hear the White Rabbit in the distance saying, "Oh, my ears and whiskers!" and "I'm so late!"

Alice ran faster, so fast that it took her by surprise when the tunnel floor suddenly dropped away and she dropped with it—*WHOOSH*—straight down.

Falling is usually kind of scary, but this was a very long, slow, floaty fall. Alice was actually quite comfortable.

She twirled and did her ballet positions, which were much more fun to do without Ms. Asia frowning at her form. She noticed that she

was falling past all sorts of interesting things on the tunnel walls—maps, posters of the constellations, even photos of her favorite TV scientist.

This place seems pretty cool, thought Alice as she kept falling. She even had time to grab a few things as she descended, and put them in her pockets: a hand mirror, a headband, a thimble.

Dinah would love this too thought Alice. Since cats are not exactly fond of falls, that probably wasn't true. Alice didn't see any mice, which Dinah *was* fond of, but she thought this was the sort of place that might have a bat or two. *Bats are just mice with wings*, thought Alice. (Again, not really.)

But as she fell and fell, she wondered over and over: *Do cats eat bats? Do cats eat bats?* and even *Do bats eat cats?* She couldn't answer the questions either way. Finally, she hit the bottom with a solid thump that didn't hurt a bit.

Jumping up, Alice caught a glimpse of the White Rabbit's tail as it turned a corner. She hurried after it into a hallway, but when she got there, it was gone.

As she tried to figure out what to do next, Alice saw that she was in a room with many doors of all different sizes and colors. She tried to open them, but they were all locked.

"So annoying," she muttered to herself, since there was no one else to mutter to. She added some extra-hard foot stomping, just because she could. That was the kind of thing her sister would have complained about. But Serena wasn't there, so Alice felt free to stomp as hard and loud as she wanted to. It wasn't as much fun as she thought it would be, and a tingle at the back of her neck made her stop and turn around.

A pretty little glass table stood in the middle of the room, and a gleaming gold key sat on top. Alice snatched it up and tried it in each locked door, until she got to the smallest one—and the key fit!

Alice opened the door. She was too big to fit through, so she bent down to take a peek—and saw the most gorgeous garden she'd ever seen:

rolling hills, sunflowers, and waterfalls. If only she could get herself small enough to fit through that tiny door!

"There's got to be a way," said Alice, shutting the door. Because after chasing a talking, vest-wearing, watch-holding rabbit down a hole and finding a gold key, Alice figured there's always a way to do just about anything.

The tingly feeling came back, and Alice whirled around again.

A pretty little bottle sat on the table. Its label said DRINK ME in fancy letters.

Now, Alice had almost made the honor roll last semester, so she was smart enough to know that she shouldn't drink from any old bottle just because it told her to. And before Serena had gotten so boring, she'd read Alice stories of silly children who didn't listen and drank from bottles without realizing their labels said POISON.

Alice looked all over the bottle. It didn't say POISON anywhere. Satisfied, she opened it and drank. It was just like a cup of hot chocolate—no, soda!—no, lemonade! It tasted like all kinds of good things, and she drank down to the last drop.

As she smacked her lips, she noticed that the table in front of her seemed to be getting bigger and bigger. Soon it was the size of a building!

She turned, and now the door was so big that she couldn't even reach the doorknob. She was shrinking! Alice curled herself up into a ball, but realizing that it might not stop her from shrinking away into nothing, she stood up with her hands on her hips.

Finally, she stopped shrinking, and Alice stomped her foot hard to make sure she was still there. She was definitely small enough to get through the door, but too small to hold the now *ginormous* gold key!

Alice started to cry.

When she paused to wipe her face with the skirt of her dress (Serena wasn't around to scold), she noticed that there was now a lovely little cake on the table.

The cake was dusted with sugar and dotted with candies that spelled EAT ME across the top. Alice was smart enough to know that cake is always a good thing, so she didn't hesitate. She climbed up to the tabletop and took a bite.

And another. And another.

It was very good cake.

"I think...I'm growing!" said Alice, hopping off the table and standing beside it. "Curiouser and curiouser!" (All the interesting happenings had jumbled up her words a little.)

She grew and grew until she had to fold herself up to fit in the room. And that meant that, once again, she was too big to get through the door.

"Oh, my ears and whiskers, I'm so late!" said a familiar voice in the distance. With some difficulty, Alice turned and caught a glimpse of the White Rabbit.

"Help!" she called out. And the White Rabbit, who really had not expected to see a giant girl, shrieked and ran off, dropping a little fan and a pair of gloves as it hopped away.

Thinking that this really was the fanciest rabbit she'd ever seen, Alice picked up the fan. She swished it around, and she felt herself getting smaller!

With the fan in her hand, Alice shrank and shrank. She quickly dropped it before she shrank away to nothing. Then she wondered what would have happened if she had. Could she shrink to nothing? Would she know if she were nothing? Would she still even be Alice? Maybe she had already become someone else! Maybe she had turned into Marie Phillips, who gossiped and tended to pick her nose when she thought no one was looking. This kind of thinking was very confusing, so Alice started to say her times tables to herself just to clear her head.

"Well, I'm not Marie," she said after quickly getting through the four, seven, nine, and twelve times tables. Marie had trouble past the twos. But Alice might be Tara Dodgson, who was very good at math and even gave herself extra-credit problems, which Alice found slightly annoying.

It was all too much. Everything in this strange place was *a lot*—even Alice's tears were too. She cried again until she thought she'd used up a lifetime's worth of tears. And that made her cry more. After a while, she realized that she was crying *and* treading water.

She had cried an ocean of tears!

Alice was a good swimmer, so she didn't panic. She tucked the little gold key into her pocket and started swimming toward the door.

Splash! A mouse joined her in the water. It looked rather big, but that was probably because she was rather small.

"Hello!" she said.

"Hi," said the Mouse. "Who are you?"

Alice wished she had thought to ask that first. "Well, I'm pretty sure I was Alice when I woke up this morning, but now . . .a lot has changed, so I'm not quite sure."

"I don't like change," said the Mouse. "I don't understand where all this water came from."

Alice didn't want to mention the crying, so she changed the subject. "You have lovely fur," she said. "Just like my cat, Dinah."

"*Cat!*" squeaked the Mouse, scrambling away.

Oops. Alice had forgotten that even though a cat might enjoy the sight of a mouse, mice don't usually feel the same way. Mice usually run far, far away from cats.

"I didn't mean to bring up a . . .sensitive topic," said Alice quickly. "How about dogs? I've been asking for one, but—"

The Mouse kept going.

"Wait, wait! Please don't leave! I won't talk at all!"

The Mouse paused. "Fine," it said, giving Alice a considerable amount of side-eye. "Let's swim to shore and *not* talk about . . .those who shall not be named."

As they started off, Alice heard more splashes and looked around. They had company. A duck, a baby eagle, even a dodo bird, which looked exactly the way Alice would have imagined a dodo would look, if she'd imagined dodos. With lots of splashing, they all swam to dry ground.

Soaked and dripping, Alice and the animals sat on the shore.

"How will we get dry?" asked the baby eagle.

"I'll tell a story," said the Mouse. "It's the driest thing I know." The Mouse cleared its throat. "Once upon a time, a time that was once but not

again, a time upon a time of all time, a time that was found advisable to . . ."

The Mouse went on and on, and everyone got very bored and stayed very wet.

The Dodo interrupted. "Let's run a race," it said. "That will work." The Dodo started running about in circles, wings flapping. The other animals followed, and after a shrug, so did Alice. Even the Mouse, who was a little offended, did too. In a few minutes, they were dry.

"Hooray!" shouted the Mouse, who seemed to be in a much better mood. "Who won?"

Everyone looked at the Dodo. The Dodo looked at Alice.

"*She'll* decide," said the Dodo. All the animals looked expectantly at Alice.

"Who won? Who won?" they cried.

"Um, we all did?" said Alice. "We all did!" she said again, like she meant it.

"Hooray! Hooray!" yelled the animals. "Prizes! Prizes!"

Alice reached into a pocket of her dress and took out all the things she'd grabbed on her way down the rabbit hole. She had just enough—one for each animal.

"Hooray!" they all cried again.

"But what about you?" said the Dodo.

"Where's your prize?"

Alice checked her other pocket and found a gum wrapper. She held it up, and the animals cheered, even the Mouse. Everyone said good-bye, and soon Alice was alone again.

chapter 3

*T**hat was fun*, Alice thought. Then she heard *tap-tap-tapp*ing footsteps and looked up. It was the White Rabbit!

"Oh, my fur and whiskers! Where could I have dropped them?" it muttered.

Alice realized the White Rabbit was searching

for the fan and gloves, but when she looked around, they, along with the table, the bottle, even the ocean of tears, had all disappeared.

"Mary Ann!" called the White Rabbit, looking directly at Alice. "What on earth are you doing here?"

That's what I'd like to know, thought Alice. "I'm not—" she started.

"Go and fetch me a new pair of gloves and a fan right away. I'm late for the party!"

Alice was so flustered that she just nodded and ran off immediately.

"It sure is bossy," grumbled Alice. But she did lose its fan and gloves, so she hurried along. After a while, she came to a small house that had a sign that said w. RABBIT nearby the front door.

Well, that's helpful, thought Alice, wishing her exams could be this way instead of having questions like how many dogs were needed to cook seventeen carrots at a busy intersection.

The front door was unlocked, and since she had been *ordered* there, Alice went right inside. She found a fan and gloves very quickly (the White Rabbit was very organized), and just as she was about to leave, she saw a bottle on the kitchen table.

It didn't say DRINK ME, but it didn't say POISON, either.

"I know something interesting happens when I eat or drink anything here. I'll see what this little bottle does. I wouldn't mind getting a little bigger again," said Alice to herself. "Then that fancy White Rabbit might listen to me." So she drank.

Immediately, she grew. And grew. And— *yikes*—GREW!

She didn't stop growing until she was almost

too big for the house. She tried to bend and fold and make herself comfortable. (It wasn't working.) Then Alice heard voices outside.

"Mary Ann! What are you doing in there?" It was the White Rabbit. "What is taking so long?"

"I'm…a bit stuck!" she called out.

"Whoa," said a voice. "Is that her leg?"

"The door's locked!" cried another voice. "I say we knock it down!"

"But…my door—" the White Rabbit began, but it was drowned out by a chorus of "Break it down!"

Alice heard someone scrabbling up the side of the house. Quickly, she stuck her giant hand out the window and grabbed. The White Rabbit was climbing up to the windowsill, but when it saw Alice's giant hand, it shrieked and jumped to the ground.

"Let's send Bill in," she heard it say, gasping for breath.

"Bill! Bill! Bill!" chanted the other voices.

Alice wondered how Bill felt about this. She also wondered who Bill was.

A few moments later, she heard someone (probably Bill) coming down the chimney. Alice used her huge leg to give a powerful *kick*!

Her foot made contact with an unfortunate bottom, sending the intruder right back up and out the chimney. She heard a thud as probably-Bill landed on the grass in front of the house.

That should do it, thought Alice. There were murmurs outside, then silence.

Ping! Ping! Pebbles suddenly hit the house from all directions. Some flew in through the window.

"Stop it right now!" Alice yelled in her best evil-monster voice.

And they did. Alice looked at the pebbles that had made it onto the floor and realized they had turned into tiny cakes.

Well, I can't get any bigger, Alice thought as she picked one up. And it *was* cake, after all. She ate it in one bite.

She was shrinking again!

Alice ate the tiny cakes until she was just small enough to leave the White Rabbit's house through the front door. As she marched out with her head held high, she noticed a lizard rubbing its backside. *That must be Bill*, she thought.

She whirled around, giving the group of rabbits, lizards, birds, and guinea pigs a hard stare, but they stared back even harder and rushed toward her.

Uh-oh, she thought.

She turned and ran.

After a while, Alice slowed to a walk. She needed to think. "I must get back to my normal size," she said aloud, "if I can even remember what that was....And I must find that beautiful garden, or this whole adventure will have been for nothing!"

Alice walked a little more and bumped right into a mushroom that was as tall as she was. She walked all around it. Then a voice from above said calmly, "Who, exactly, are you?"

Alice looked up. A giant blue caterpillar sat on top of the mushroom.

Why can't anything just be regular-sized? thought Alice. *But maybe this is regular for this place! I wish I knew where this place was!*

The Caterpillar sighed and folded its arms.

"Oh! Sorry!" said Alice. "I'm Alice. At least, I was this morning. It could be different depending on where here is." She'd learned about time zones in Geography. "Is now morning?"

"You don't sound very sure of yourself," said

the Caterpillar.

"You wouldn't, either," shot back Alice, "falling and growing and shrinking all over the place like I have! Now I just want to grow to a good, normal size."

The Caterpillar crawled down and stood upright next to Alice. It was exactly her current height. "You're my size," it said coldly. "I find this size perfectly fine." It started to stomp away, which was quite effective since it had so many legs.

Oops, thought Alice. Wherever she was, it was a place where everyone sure was touchy. "Wait!" she called.

The Caterpillar stopped. They looked at each other. "I'm waiting for you to explain," said the Caterpillar.

"Explain what?"

"Yourself."

"But that's what I'm saying—I can't explain myself. I'm all turned round!"

"Then maybe you should turn straight," said the Caterpillar.

"I'd like to see how you feel after you spend some time in your cocoon and then come out a butterfly. You might be a little discomboo—discombay—"

"Discombobulated," said the Caterpillar. "You're not a word wizard, that's for sure."

"Excuse me?" asked Alice.

"You arc," said the Caterpillar.

"I am what?"

"That's exactly what I'd like to know," said the Caterpillar.

"Just who do you think you are?" asked Alice. This was what she heard her dad ask whenever he was losing an argument.

"A caterpillar," said the Caterpillar. "And who, may I ask again, are *you?*"

"But we've come full circle!" cried Alice.

"So you might as well know," said the Caterpillar, walking away, "one side makes you grow smaller, and the other side makes you grow taller."

Side of what? thought Alice.

"The mushroom," said the Caterpillar, as if she'd asked her question aloud. And it was soon out of sight.

Alice stared at the huge mushroom. Its round top didn't have sides! Now what?

chapter 4

Alice did something especially clever. She stretched each arm around the mushroom, hugged it tight, and plucked off a bit in each hand.

First she took a bite from her left hand—and she started shrinking! Quickly, she popped a bite from her right hand into her mouth, and she grew. She alternated bites until she was back to what she thought was her old size. Then she set off to find the garden once and for all.

Mushroom bites and tiny cakes weren't exactly filling, so after more walking, Alice was ready for a pizza, or a triple cheeseburger, or even a big cake (because, after all, cake is cake).

She spotted a house in the distance, with curls of smoke winding out of the chimney. It had the cozy look of a fairy-tale house. Maybe there was gingerbread inside! A frog-faced man wearing a curly white wig and a fancy uniform stood in front. He had a very serious expression on his face that made him look decidedly silly.

A fish-faced man, in an even curlier wig, approached Frog-face. Fish-face held a large envelope. "For the Duchess," he said, handing

Frog-face the envelope. Then they both bowed very low to each other, so low that their wings got all curled up and tangled together! They looked so ridiculous that Alice had to laugh. She laughed so hard that she ran to hide. Finally, Fish-face disentangled himself and left.

Alice walked over to Frog-face, who now sipped a cup of tea. A lot of noise came from inside the house.

"Uh, do you think everything's all right in there?" she asked Frog-face, who continued to sip

his tea. "Is this the Duchess's house? I heard that she might be having an . . .event?" Alice went on. "I imagine there will be food, right?"

Frog-face carefully set his teacup onto the saucer just as a loud *crash!* and a yell came from inside. "I guess you heard *that*," he said.

Alice raised her hand to knock.

"Don't bother knocking," said Frog-face. "You can hear them, so they can't hear you." He picked up his tea and sipped again.

Alice opened the door and went inside.

Crash! A plate smashed the wall just behind her head.

"Hey!" she yelled. "Watch what you're doing!" But no one was listening. A woman in a frilly dress and a fancy hat stood holding a very wriggly and fussy baby. *That must be the Duchess*, Alice thought. A cook stirred a big pot of something on the stove. Alice moved closer. It smelled good, but it also—

"*Achoo!*" sneezed Alice. The Duchess sneezed too. So did the baby. The Cook just stirred harder, and a very large cat sitting in the middle of the room didn't sneeze, either. It grinned a big, wide grin, from ear to ear. Which, on a cat, was a little strange to see.

"Excuse me, Your, uh…Duchessness," said Alice. "Why is your cat grinning like that?"

"Because—*achoo!*—it's a Cheshire Cat, of course," sniffed the Duchess.

"Ohhh-kay," said Alice. "I guess I didn't know."

"You must not know much of anything," said the Duchess.

I know that dress is ugly, thought Alice. But she knew better than to be rude out loud to adults,

so she just took a deep breath. Mistake. *"Achoo!"*

The cook stopped stirring, and Alice was much relieved—until a brass pot whizzed past her head. The cook began throwing pots, pans, and dishes across the room. The Cheshire Cat just sat and grinned. Alice ducked, and the Duchess ran over and thrust the baby into her arms.

"I'm out of here!" yelled the Duchess as a teapot knocked her hat off. She raced from the room.

Alice, clutching the baby, swerved out of the way of a wooden spoon and zipped through the front door. Frog-face still sat there, sipping his tea, but he definitely had an "I told you so" look in his eyes.

"Well, at least I got you out of that dangerous house," Alice said to the baby.

The baby grunted back loudly and wriggled.

"We're safe! Don't fuss, poor little thing," said Alice. She pushed the baby's bonnet out of the way so that she could comfort its cute little baby nose.

Only the baby's nose was not exactly cute or little. It was decidedly...snouty. And the baby's eyes were very small and squinty. Alice realized what she was holding.

"A pig!"

She quickly put the pig on the ground. Its grunts became happy as it trotted away.

"Good thing it turned out to be a pig," said Alice to herself. "I wasn't going to say anything out loud, but it was *not* a cute baby!" When she realized that she was saying it out loud, Alice felt guilty and vowed to say one hundred kind things to Marie when she got back from . . .wherever she was.

Alice looked around, wondering which way to go next, and was surprised to see the grinning Cheshire Cat perched on a tree branch nearby. Since it seemed so pleasant, Alice walked over. *And I'll be extra-polite*, she thought. She was still feeling guilty about what she'd said about the pig-baby, and also the cat had pretty sharp claws and teeth.

"Excuse me, Most Honorable Cheshire Cat, which way should I go?"

"Where do you want to go?" asked the Cat.

"I don't much care where—"

"Then it doesn't matter which way you go," said the Cat, swishing its tail.

"—as long as I get somewhere," finished Alice.

"You'll certainly do that if you walk long enough," said the Cat.

Alice couldn't argue with that, even though she really wanted to. "Who else lives around here?" she asked.

"That way is the Mad Hatter," said the Cat,

pointing to the right. "And that way is the March Hare," it continued, pointing left. "You can visit either one. They're both mad."

"But I don't want to hang out with mad people," said Alice. "I like smiles, like yours." She congratulated herself on getting that in.

"Too late. We're all mad here, including you," said the Cat.

"What makes you think I'm mad?"

"Well, you're here, aren't you?" replied the Cat. And then it grinned even bigger.

Alice opened her mouth, then closed it.

"Are you coming to the Queen's party?" asked the Cat. "Everyone who's anyone will be there."

"I'd love to," said Alice, "but I wasn't invited."

"Oh well," said the Cat. "I'll be there." Suddenly, it vanished.

"Okay, bye," said Alice to the air.

The Cat reappeared. "I almost forgot. What happened to the baby?"

"It was actually a pig," said Alice with a shrug.

"I figured that," said the Cat. And then it slowly faded away, bit by bit, until all that was left was the big grin. The grin hung in the air for a while, and then it too, disappeared.

Well, that was kind of creepy. Alice shuddered. "I've seen lots of cats without a grin—cats are pretty grumpy—but a grin without a cat!" She shuddered again.

Since it was May (or at least it had been before she'd gone down the rabbit hole), she decided to go toward the March Hare's house. *March was two months ago*, she thought, *so maybe it's a little less mad now.*

She approached a house with bunny ear–shaped chimneys and a fur-thatched roof, and she got a little nervous. The house was quite big, so she ate a few bits of right-hand mushroom in order to grow a bit. Then she took a deep breath and stepped forward.

chapter 5

There was a lovely long table under a tree in front of the house, and it turned out that both the Mad Hatter and the March Hare were there, having tea. A dormouse sat between them, fast asleep. They were all bunched up together at one end of the table.

Alice's stomach rumbled.

"No room! No room!" the Mad Hatter and the March Hare cried as Alice walked closer.

"Don't be silly," said Alice, sitting down. "There's plenty of room."

"Would you like a scone?" asked the Mad Hatter. He had one hat stacked on top of another on his head, a purple velvet suit, and a necklace of thimbles. *Interesting sense of fashion in this place*, thought Alice.

"Oh, yes, please!" she said. Now, *this* was more like it.

"We don't have any scones," said the March Hare.

Alice's stomach rumbled again. "It wasn't very nice of you to offer," she said.

"It wasn't very nice of you to just sit down uninvited," said the March Hare.

"B-but there really is a lot of extra room," Alice sputtered.

"Your hair looks hilarious," said the Mad Hatter. The March Hare nodded.

Alice reached up. Her half-done braids had unraveled when she'd fallen down the rabbit hole. "That's extremely rude," she snapped.

"Why is a raven like a writing desk?" asked the Mad Hatter.

Alice leaned forward. "Ooh, riddles! I can do this one."

"You mean you can find out the answer?" asked the Hatter.

"Yes, exactly," said Alice.

"Then you should say what you mean," said the Hatter. The March Hare nodded.

"I do—I mean what I say! It's the same thing," said Alice.

"Is 'I see what I eat' the same as 'I eat what I see'?" asked the Hatter. "I think not." The March Hare shook his head.

"Or 'I like what I get' the same as 'I get what I like'?" the March Hare asked.

"Or 'I breathe when I sleep' the same as 'I sleep when I breathe'?" murmured the Dormouse.

"That *is* the same for *you*," said the Hatter. He poured some tea on the Dormouse's nose.

"Yes, exactly," murmured the Dormouse. Then he started snoring.

The Hatter looked at his pocket watch. "What day is it?" he said, shaking it.

"The fourth," said Alice after a quick think.

"I knew it!" said the Hatter. "My watch is two days off!" Disgusted, he handed it to the March Hare, who dipped the watch in a cup of tea.

"Your watch tells days, not time?" asked Alice.

"Why not?" asked the Hatter. "Did you guess the riddle yet?"

"I give up," said Alice. "So why is a raven like a writing desk?"

"How should I know?" The Hatter shrugged. So did the Hare.

Alice opened her mouth, then closed it again.

"Tell us a story!" said the March Hare to Alice.

"Uh…," Alice stuttered. "I don't know a good one."

"Then the Dormouse shall!" cried the other two. And they pinched the Dormouse awake.

"I wasn't asleep," said the Dormouse. "I heard everything. Very interesting."

"Just tell us a story before you fall asleep again," said the March Hare.

"Yes, please do," Alice chimed in. She was hoping they'd bring out sandwiches, or even just a cracker, if she was polite.

"Once upon a time," said the Dormouse, "there were three sisters living at the bottom of a well."

"What did they eat?" asked Alice.

"Treacle," said the Dormouse.

"They'd probably get sick, just eating syrup all the time," said Alice.

"They did. Quite sick," replied the Dormouse.

"So where did the treacle come from, if they lived at the bottom of a well?" asked Alice.

The Dormouse frowned. "It was a treacle well."

"There's no such thing!" Alice burst out. How many impossible things was she expected to believe—especially on an empty stomach?

"Why don't you have some more tea?" said the March Hare to Alice.

"I haven't had *any*, so I can't exactly have *more*," snapped Alice. (She was really hungry.)

"You mean you can't have less," said the Hatter. "You can always have more than nothing."

"You stay out of this!" said Alice.

"*Now* who's the rude one?" said the Hatter.

"I can't tell a story if you keep interrupting," said the Dormouse primly.

"Sorry! I'm sorry!" said Alice. "I promise I won't interrupt again."

"Ahem," said the Dormouse. "So, the sisters were learning to draw, and—"

"Draw what?" interrupted Alice, forgetting her promise.

"Treacle," said the Dormouse, very slowly.

"I want a clean cup," said the Hatter. "Let's move one place on."

So they all moved over just one seat. Alice ended up at the March Hare's old seat, which was kind of a bummer because the Hare had knocked a jug of milk onto his plate.

"*Anyway*, they drew things that began with *M*," the Dormouse went on, settling down into its new seat.

"Why with an *M*?" asked Alice.

"Why not?" said the March Hare.

"They drew mousetraps...the moon..." The Dormouse's voice grew softer. "Muchness." It began to snore.

"I don't think—" began Alice.

"Then you definitely shouldn't talk," said the Hatter. And he high-fived the March Hare over the Dormouse's head.

How rude, thought Alice. She jumped up and stalked away from the table, wondering if they'd apologize and ask her to return.

They didn't.

When she looked back, the March Hare and Hatter were trying to stuff the Dormouse into a teapot.

"Worst tea party ever!" Alice muttered, and kept walking. Then she spotted a tree with a door in it.

Very curious, she thought. Considering the way everything else had gone today, it seemed to Alice that the best thing to do would be to open the door and go inside. So she did.

chapter 6

She was back in the first hallway, and the gold key was sitting on top of the table!

Alice grabbed the key, unlocked the door, and ate a bite of shrinking mushroom. Finally, she stepped through the door into the most beautiful garden she'd ever seen. Sunflowers, poppies, and daffodils mingled with strawberry plants and grapevines. The sky was the bluest of blues, and the birds weren't just twecting—they were singing like a feathery choir.

Three gardeners, who were dressed as playing cards, painted white roses red.

"Why are you doing that?" asked Alice.

The gardeners looked around nervously. Then one whispered, "We were supposed to plant a red rosebush. If the queen sees white roses, it'll be off

with our heads. She hates white roses."

"Oh, no! She's coming!" said another. All three gardeners fell flat and facedown.

Alice's eyes grew wide at the sound of marching feet. She'd never seen a real live queen before!

A long procession of royals and guests, all dressed as playing cards, came forward. There were soldiers, assistants, friends, children, and even animal guests. Alice caught a glimpse of the White Rabbit, who looked more nervous than ever. Finally, the Jack of Hearts passed by, followed by the King and Queen of Hearts.

Alice wasn't sure if she should curtsy.

The Queen stopped in front of her and glared. "Who are *you*?" she bellowed. Her bright red dress was almost too red for Alice to look at. Her crown had a big heart on top, but she didn't seem very loving.

"I'm Alice, Your Majesty," said Alice, bowing just in case.

"And them?" The Queen pointed toward the gardeners, who were still facedown on the ground.

"How should I know?" said Alice, surprised by her own courage. "I'm trying to mind my own business."

"Off with her head!" screamed the Queen, her face turning a shade of red so bright that Alice really did have to look away.

"That's nonsense," said Alice.

"She's just a little girl, dear," said the King in a low voice.

The Queen huffed and ordered the Jack to turn the gardeners over so she could identify them. "What have you been doing?" she asked them.

"We—" started one.

"Aha! I see! Off with their heads!" she called out, and marched on with the rest of the procession.

"Don't worry, I got you," Alice whispered to the gardeners when the Queen was out of earshot. She hid them in a large flowerpot.

The Queen turned around. "Are their heads off?" she asked.

The soldiers looked around and, not seeing the gardeners, said, "Yes, their heads are gone."

"Do you play croquet?" yelled the Queen.

Alice looked around. When no one else answered, she said, "Wait, are you talking to me? Sure, yes!"

She had watched a lot of baseball with her parents and wondered if it was pretty much the same thing.

"Come on, then!" shouted the Queen.

So Alice joined the procession, hoping they'd grab a bite to eat before the match.

"It's a very fine day," whispered a voice at her side. It was the White Rabbit!

"Very!" said Alice, glad to have a buddy of sorts. "Where's the Duchess?"

"Shhhh!" whispered the Rabbit. "She got here late, accidentally-on-purpose kicked the Queen— it was a mess." His voice got even lower. "And now it's going to be, you know, off with her head."

Alice snorted loudly, ignoring the Rabbit's shushing.

They arrived at the croquet grounds, which were full of hills and valleys and nooks and crannies. The soldiers immediately bent themselves into arches. *Maybe this isn't like baseball after all,* thought Alice.

Then everyone got mallets, which were live flamingos, and balls, which were live hedgehogs!

This is just too weird, even for this place, thought Alice as she gently tried to hold her flamingo by its long legs. The flamingo turned around to look at her in a puzzled "What in the world do you think you're doing?" way that made Alice laugh out loud. The hedgehogs did not sit in quiet rolled-up balls, because hedgehogs, like Alice, are not stupid. They just unrolled themselves and walked away, exploring the grounds.

Everyone was playing at the same time, running and tripping and trying to catch flamingos and hedgehogs. They bickered and bumped into one another until the Queen started shouting, "Off with her head! Off with his head!" every few moments.

Alice didn't like all that beheading. It was just rude. She didn't mind the Queen's stomping around, and that crown was pretty sweet, but still. "There won't be anybody left if the Queen has her way!"

As she wondered how to make an escape, an enormous grin appeared in the air nearby.

"Cheshire Cat!" Alice said, happy to have someone—at least someone's mouth—to chat with.

"How's it going?" asked the Cat's mouth. Slowly, the eyes, ears, and whole head appeared.

Alice put down her flamingo. "This game is ridiculous and unfair!" she began. "There aren't any rules and I can't hear myself think, much less get a word in edgewise."

The Cat's head nodded. "What do you think of the Queen?"

"Well, she's—" Alice realized that the Queen was very close. "She's definitely going to win!" Alice finished with a large, fake grin of her own.

The Queen smiled and strolled away. Her hedgehog waddled off in the other direction.

"Who are you talking to?" asked the King, walking over.

"Allow me to introduce the Cheshire Cat," said Alice, feeling like an insider for once.

"You may kiss my hand," said the King to the Cat.

"Nah, I'm good," said the Cat.

"*What?!*" said the King. He spun around. "My Queen! Have this Cat removed immediately!"

The Queen didn't even look over. "Off with its head," she said half-heartedly. Everyone was now running around in circles, and the flamingos and hedgehogs had all escaped.

Alice fought her way through the confusion until she was back next to the Cat. There was a large crowd around it, and much shouting. Someone wondered if you could really say "off with its head" if all there was *was* a head. The King argued that the presence of a head settled that question. They continued this rather gruesome argument back and forth, until Alice said, "Let the Duchess settle this. It's *her* Cat."

While the soldiers went off to get the Duchess, the Cat wisely used the opportunity to fade away. By the time they returned, the Cat had completely disappeared. The King and soldiers ran off to find it.

The Duchess linked arms with Alice and smiled. "So great to see you again!" she said.

Maybe it was the pepper that made her so awful before, thought Alice. *Maybe pepper is what makes*

*people ill-tempered! And vinegar makes them sour,
and sugar makes them sweet!* That last one seemed
like her most important discovery.

She felt a jab on her shoulder. The Duchess
was resting her (extremely pointy) chin on it.

"Excuse you," Alice muttered. But she didn't
want to be rude, so she added, "It looks like the
game's going well," which wasn't at all true, but
it was polite.

"The trial is starting!" someone yelled.

"What trial?" Alice asked, but no one answered,
and she followed the crowd to a large courtroom.

The King and Queen sat in the middle of
the courtroom on splendid thrones. A crowd sat
around them. The Jack of Hearts stood before
the royals, his hands tied behind his back. A
giant tray of fruit tarts on a table in the middle of
the room caught Alice's eye.

Alice knew about trials, so she knew there'd be a judge, which seemed to be the King, since he was wearing a curly white wig.

She looked over at the jury box. Twelve different animals sat, with pencils and pads, already taking notes, even though the trial had not yet begun. Someone's pencil kept squeaking in the most annoying way, and Alice realized that it was Bill the lizard's.

"Of course it's Bill," Alice muttered. She snuck up behind him and snatched the pencil away so quickly that he didn't realize it was gone. He just kept writing with his finger, which obviously didn't work. *Oh, Bill,* Alice thought.

The White Rabbit blew a trumpet and unrolled a scroll. "Silence in the court!" it called out. It read:

The Queen of Hearts,

she made some tarts,

all on a summer's day;

The Knave of Hearts,

he stole those tarts,

and took them clean away.

Alice was very pleased with herself for knowing that the "Knave" was the Jack.

"Verdict now, jury!" yelled the King.

"Uh, there's a process before that part," said the Rabbit.

"Yeah, okay," said the King. "First witness!"

The Hatter came forward, holding a teacup in one hand and a slice of buttered toast in the other. "Sorry for the food," he said. "I hadn't finished my tea."

"When did you start?"

"March fourteenth?" said the Hatter.

"Fifteenth," said the March Hare from behind him.

"Sixteenth," said the Dormouse from behind the Hare.

The jurors wrote down all the numbers and added and divided them. Bill looked up quickly with a satisfied smile. Even without a pencil, he'd finished figuring first. *Show-off,* thought Alice. *Just like Tara Dodgson.*

"Take off your hat!" the King said.

"It's not mine—" started the Hatter.

"Thief!" yelled the King. The jurors took more notes.

"No, I mean I make them to sell," said the Hatter. "I don't keep any for my own head." He took off his hat to reveal the other underneath. "Your Honor—um—Highness."

"You'd better explain yourself if you don't want that head removed!" said the King.

The Hatter stuttered and stared at the Queen, who glared back at him. He got so nervous that he bit his teacup and tried to sip his toast.

I feel...strange, thought Alice, looking down at herself. She was getting bigger!

"Stop squeezing me!" said the Dormouse, who'd sat beside her.

"I can't help it," whispered Alice. "I'm growing!"

"That's just rude," said the Dormouse.

The Hatter started speaking. "Then the Dormouse said..." He looked over at the Dormouse, who was snoring.

"Said what?" asked the King.

"I—I don't remember," stammered the Hatter, falling to his knees in fright.

"That hat and that head are about to go," warned the King. "Stand down!"

"I'm already on the floor," whispered the Hatter.

"Then go sit down!" yelled the King, and the Hatter ran out of the courtroom.

"Just take off his head outside," said the Queen. But the Hatter was gone.

"Next witness!" called the King.

The Cook stomped forward, making everyone sneeze as she passed.

"Speak," said the King.

"Nope," said the Cook.

The King looked confused.

"Uh, maybe you should just ask a question, Your Highness," said the White Rabbit.

The King folded his arms. "What are tarts made of?"

"Pepper," barked the Cook.

"Treacle," cried the Dormouse, waking up.

"Off with its head!" shouted the Queen, pointing at the Dormouse. Everyone scurried around the room, and the Dormouse was hustled out by its friends.

"You do the next one," the King said to the Queen. "My head hurts."

Not as much as it would if it was taken off, thought Alice as she watched the Rabbit look down at its list. She jumped in surprise when it called out, "Alice!"

chapter 7

Alice stepped forward. Since she was still growing, her steps were more like stomps in the tiny courtroom. "What do you have to say about all this?" asked the King.

"Nothing," said Alice.

"That's important," the King said to the jury.

"Write it down." They did. Bill finger-wrote for a long time.

"Unimportant, you mean, sir," said the White Rabbit.

"Yes, that's what I meant," said the King. So the jury wrote that down too. "Unimportant, important, unimportant, important," chanted the King.

Alice rolled her eyes.

"Silence!" shouted the King, who was the only one talking. He nodded at Alice. "Go on with your story."

"I didn't start one," said Alice. "I wouldn't even know *where* to start anyway."

"Begin at the beginning," the King said, "and go till you come to the end, and stop."

Alice just looked at him until he looked away.

The King picked up a book and read aloud.

"'Rule Forty-Two: Anyone taller than a mile high must be removed from the court.'" He slammed the book down and looked up at Alice.

"Don't look at me," she said. "I'm not a mile high."

"Are too," said the King.

"I'm not going anywhere," said Alice. "You just made that up." Plus that tray of yummy tarts was so close.

"It's the oldest rule in the book," said the King.

"Then it would be Rule Number One, not Forty-Two," said Alice, wishing someone were close enough for a high five on that one.

The King's mouth dropped open. Then he turned to the jury. "Verdict!" he screamed.

"Uh, there's still more," said the Rabbit. "We have some evidence. . .a letter from the Jack to... somebody."

"Or nobody," said the King, looking as if he was about to start chanting again.

The White Rabbit quickly opened the letter and said, "Oh, it's not a letter. It's a poem!"

"I didn't write it!" said the Jack. "There's no proof! There's no name signed at the end!"

"Aha!" said the King. "If you hadn't been trying to be sneaky, you would have signed it!"

"Guilty!" cried the Queen. "Off with his head!"

"You didn't prove a thing," scoffed Alice, who was now her regular size and feeling very bold.

"You be quiet!" said the Queen.

"No!" Alice yelled back.

"Off with her head!" screamed the Queen.

"I don't have to listen to you at all," said Alice. "You're just a pack of cards!"

Suddenly, all the card-shaped spectators in the courtroom rose up in the air and flew at Alice's head. As she waved her arms and tried to beat them away, she tripped backward and fell...

...into the lap of her sister, Serena, who was putting finishing touches of flower blossoms in the last braid.

"Just in time," said Serena. "I'm finished!"

"I had such a curious dream," said Alice, yawning. And she told her sister the whole thing. Serena smiled and nodded, only half listening.

So Alice decided that she'd write it all down so that everyone could read it. She'd make her own book. *After all*, she thought, *everyone knows there's nothing better than a really good book.*

As she and Serena left the park and walked home together, Alice stuck a hand in her pocket and pulled out…a strawberry tart, only slightly squished!

ghost
writer™

FUN
AND
PUZZLES

Alice is so cool — kind, great style, friendly; we would definitely be friends in real life. Naturally, I wanted to know all about her book. Here's what I found out:

Alice is based on a real girl! Her name was Alice Liddell, and she was the daughter of Lewis Carroll's friend.

Alice's Adventures in Wonderland was written by Lewis Carroll and published in 1865. It was a huge success! (It basically went viral before viral even existed.)

Lewis Carroll is a made-up name. That's called a pseudonym. The author's real name was Charles Lutwidge Dodgson.

Lewis Carroll couldn't decide on a title. He almost called it:
Alice's Hour in Elfland
Alice's Adventure Under Ground
Alice Among the Fairies
I think Alice's Adventures in Wonderland sounds much better!!!!! Dreamy, right?

Lewis Carroll didn't plan on becoming an author. He taught math at a university. He made up the story of Wonderland to tell Alice and her two sisters on a boating trip they took together. After Alice kept asking him to tell it again and again, two years later, he finally wrote it down as a book.

The tree the Cheshire Cat sits in is based on a tree in the real Alice's backyard.
The original hand-written manuscript is at the British Museum in London. (Can you say field trip for tea time?)

Curtis's Mirror Message

Hey! Did you know that Lewis Carroll loved puzzles? Sometimes he'd send mirror-message letters to his friends. They had to hold the paper up to a mirror to decode his messages.

Can you read my letter? (Try holding it up to a mirror.)

ИI DOИИA,

ТΗΕЯΕ'Ƨ А GΗ0ƧТ ΗΑUИΤIИG ΤΗΕ Β0OΚƧΤOЯΕ!

WΗΥ? WΗO IƧ IТ? WΕ ИΕΕD ТO FIИD OUТ!

СUЯТIƧ

Mirror messages are trickier than just writing backwards. In a mirror, most letters look very different. C looks like Ɔ, and S looks like Ƨ. But some letters don't change at all. O and T and A look the same in a mirror. Do you know why? They're symmetrical. That means that if you draw a line down the center of the letter, they look the same on either side.

Letters	Mirror Images
A	A
B	ᙠ
C	Ɔ
D	ᗡ
E	Ǝ
F	Ⅎ
G	ᗞ
H	H
I	I
J	ᒐ
K	⋊
L	⅃
M	M
N	И
O	O
P	ꟼ
Q	Ọ
R	Я
S	ꙅ
T	T
U	U
V	V
W	W
X	X
Y	Y
Z	ꙅ

Practice mirror-writing the alphabet on a piece of paper. Next, try writing your name. Don't forget to start on the right side of the page, instead of the left.

Now write your own mirror message! You can send it to your friend, your brother or sister, or even your teacher.

Chevon's Curiouser and Curiouser Quiz

Let's just say there's never been a time when I wasn't curious. I've also never met a quiz I didn't like. Now that you've read the book, test your knowledge with my Curiouser and Curiouser Quiz!

1. How does Alice travel to Wonderland?

    a. through a wardrobe

    b. down a rabbit hole

    c. on a magic school bus

    d. in a spaceship

2. Alice tastes many flavors when she drinks from the bottle labeled DRINK ME. What does she *not* taste?

    a. lemonade

    b. soda

    c. vanilla

    d. hot chocolate

3. What color roses does the Queen hate?

    a. red

b. white

c. pink

d. yellow

4. Who is the judge in the trial?

    a. the Mad Hatter

    b. the White Rabbit

    c. the Queen of Hearts

    d. the King of Hearts

5. In the book, what is the answer to the riddle "Why is a raven like a writing desk?"

    a. There is no answer.

    b. They both have wings.

    c. They are both black.

    d. Neither can stand on its head.

6. Which of these animals does Alice meet first?

    a. Bill the lizard

    b. the Caterpillar

    c. the Dodo

    d. the Dormouse

Answers on page 104.

Ruben's Scramble

In Wonderland, everything is all mixed up and turned around. That's exactly how I felt when I moved to a new town and a new school. Nothing made sense at first. I was like a stranger in a strange land. (And that was on *top* of there being a ghost in my Grandpa's bookstore!)

Can you unscramble the letters below to find the names of six characters in the book?

CELRAPTRIAL _____

CHERIESH ACT _____

SUCSHED _____

DAM THEART _____

HIETW BARBTI _____

MORDOSUE _____

Answers on page 104.

The Curtis Challenge

Drumroll, please. It's time for my ultimate challenge. See how many smaller words you can make from the letters in **WONDERLAND**.

Here are a few words to get you started:

now, owl, dear, ladder

Write your answers on a piece of paper or type them on a computer. All words must be 3 or more letters. Can you score **20 points**?

Here's how to keep score

Each 3-letter word = 1 point

Each 4-letter word = 2 points

Each 5-letter word = 3 points

Each word with 6 letters or more = 4 points

Chevon's Amazing Definition Game

"You should say what you mean," the Mad Hatter says at the tea party, and Alice says, "I mean what I say!" You know what? Sometimes I come across a word while I'm reading and have no idea what it means. I know, I know. I should just look it up (that's what I would tell myself to do) but I came up with another way to learn the words. My amazing definition game!

See if you can choose the correct word to complete each sentence.

1. *Owww!* I hate getting pricked with a sharp needle when I sew. Now I wear a little metal cap called a _____ to protect my finger.

       a. thimble

       b. bramble

       c. beret

2. In class today, when I tried to give a book report, search through my backpack for a pencil, and tie my shoelace all at the same time, I felt very _____.

92

a. itchy

b. peaceful

c. discombobulated

3. I bowed to the _____ when she visited because she was royalty. She ranked one level below the king and queen.

a. principal

b. duchess

c. captain

4. Have you ever seen a _____? The fast-running, long-eared animal looks like a large rabbit.

a. hare

b. sloth

c. kitten

5. My aunt bakes small biscuit-like cakes called _____ and serves them with raspberry jam.

a. tacos

b. scones

c. ziti

6. _____ is a sticky, sweet syrup that's similar to honey.

a. Mustard

b. Coffee

c. Treacle

7. My brother Curtis rules on the basketball court, but when we play _____, a game where players use a mallet to knock a ball through a hoop, I always win.

    a. croquet

    b. cricket

    c. badminton

8. A _____ is a tiny mammal covered with sharp spines that protect it from predators. For protection, it can roll itself into a tight, prickly ball!

    a. rhinoceros

    b. Komodo dragon

    c. hedgehog

9. The group of people who decide the outcome (or the *verdict*) of a trial is called a _____.

    a. gaggle

    b. jury

    c. team

10. At first, my brother _____ at Donna when she said Alice had come out of the book. Later, he apologized for dismissing her and making fun of the idea.

a. whispered

b. scoffed

c. gargled

0–2 correct: **Time to try again.** Here's a hint: look for context clues in the sentences.

3–6 correct: **Good job!** You're on your way to being a true Word Warrior.

7–9 correct: **Vocab victory!** You're the Word Wizard!

10 correct: **Wow!** Now I know why you're called the Walking Dictionary!

Answers on page 104.

Donna Gets Crafty:
Playing Card People

I liked how the Queen had a playing card crew. In her royal court, the hearts are the royal family, the spades are the gardeners, the diamonds are noble people, and the clubs are the soldiers. I designed my own crew then lined them up my desk. Now when I'm doing homework, it's like my own personal cheering squad! You can make playing card people too—just follow my easy directions.

What you need:

- a deck of cards
- red construction paper
- red pipe cleaners
- scissors
- a black marker
- a pencil
- glue

1. Choose a heart playing card.

2. Cut a large heart a little bit larger than your playing card from the red construction paper. The easiest way to do this is to fold the paper in half. With your pencil, draw a half-heart shape along the folded edge. Cut on the line, then open your paper, and you'll have a perfect heart.

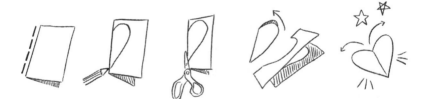

3. Fold the rounded tops of the heart down over the front of the playing card.

4. Cut a red pipe cleaner in half. Slip one half underneath the fold. Glue the card and pipe cleaner in place and let them dry.

5. Bend the pipe cleaner to make the arms.

6. Cut a small heart from the red construction paper. Turn it upside down and glue it to the top center of the playing card. Use the black marker to draw a face on the upside-down

I made a few cards from every group, then lined them up to alternate so they create a cool pattern; heart, spade, heart, spade, and diamond, club, diamond, club. —Curtis

7. To make the feet, cut two small squares the same size out of the red construction paper. Fold each one in half. Use your scissors to cut a small notch into each fold. Slip the playing card into each notch to make your card stand up.

I cut speech bubbles from white paper, then attached them to my card people's mouths. Every card had something to say, just like in my favorite graphic novels.
—Ruben

I decorated my card people with LOTS of glitter. More is more when it comes to sparkles!
—Donna

Ruben's Reading List

If you liked *Alice's Adventures in Wonderland*, I made a list of books you'll also enjoy. (Okay, okay, I'm going to fess up. It's not really *my* reading list. I had my grandpa help me. He owns Village Books, and he's a total book expert.)

The Phantom Tollbooth by Norton Juster

The Wonderful Wizard of Oz by L. Frank Baum

Charlie and the Chocolate Factory by Roald Dahl

Furthermore by Tahereh Mafi

The Serpent's Secret by Sayantani DasGupta

The Girl Who Circumnavigated Fairyland in a Ship of Her Own Making by Catherynne M. Valente

The Land of Stories: The Wishing Spell by Chris Colfer

Dragons in a Bag by Zetta Elliott

Donna's Story Starter

Reading about Alice's enchanted adventure makes me want to write a story, but I don't know what it should be about. Has this ever happened to you? My teacher once told me that one way to come up with a good story idea is to start with the words "What if...?"

Here's a "what if..." just for you!
In Wonderland, Alice drinks a potion from a bottle and shrinks. What if you suddenly became tiny? What adventures would you have?

_____

_____

_____

_____

_____

_____

_____

_____

Ghostwriter's Secret Message

Shhhh! Ghostwriter has a secret message just for you.

Here's how you can find it:

1. The first three words in Chapter Three: _____ _____ _____

2. In Chapter Two, go to the seventh word in the third paragraph: _____

3. In Chapter Five, go to the eighth word in the fourth paragraph: _____

4. In Chapter Two, find the tenth and eleventh words in the third sentence of the fourth paragraph: _____ _____

5. In Chapter One, go to the sixth word of the first sentence: _____

6. In Chapter Six, find the second-to-last paragraph and go to the word before "head hurts": _____

7. In Chapter Seven, find the last word of the eighth paragraph: _____

Write the words in order on a piece of paper to read the secret message:

_____ _____ _____ _____ _____ _____ _____ _____

_____ _____....

Answers on page 104.

103

Answers

Curtis's Mirror Message:

HI DONNA,

THERE'S A GHOST HAUNTING THE BOOKSTORE!

WHY? WHO IS IT? WE NEED TO FIND OUT!

CURTIS

Chevon's Curiouser and Curiouser Quiz: 1. b, 2. c, 3. b, 4. d, 5. a, 6. c

Ruben's Scramble: Caterpillar, Cheshire Cat, Duchess, Mad Hatter, White Rabbit, Dormouse

Chevon's Amazing Definition Game: 1. a, 2. c, 3. b, 4. a, 5. b, 6. c, 7. a, 8. c, 9. b, 10. b

Ghostwriter's Secret Message: That was fun but there's much more to my story....

About the Authors

Lewis Carroll's real name was Charles Lutwidge Dodgson. He was born in 1832 in Daresbury, England. While teaching mathematics at Oxford University, he made up stories for his friend's three daughters. The story he told the little girl named Alice and her sisters became *Alice's Adventures in Wonderland*. He had it published as a book in 1865.

Olugbemisola Rhuday-Perkovich made up stories for her little sister when she was young, including one "true story" that she'd starred on Sesame Street, but had turned herself invisible to viewers. Today, she writes fiction and nonfiction, including the NAACP Image Award nominee *Two Naomis*, with Audrey Vernick, and its sequel, Nerdy Book Club winner *Naomis Too*. She's the author of *8th Grade Superzero*, a Notable Book for a Global Society; *Someday Is Now: Clara Luper and the 1958 Oklahoma City Sit-ins*, a Notable Social Studies Trade Book for Young People; and *Above and Beyond: NASA's Journey to Tomorrow*, as well as the editor of *The Hero Next Door*, a middle grade anthology from We Need Diverse Books. She lives with her family in NYC, where she writes, makes things, and needs to get more sleep.